FIRST DELIGHTS

A Book About the Five Senses

By Tasha Tudor

PLATT & MUNK, PUBLISHERS • *New York*
A DIVISION OF GROSSET & DUNLAP

Sally lives on a farm. As the
seasons change from winter to
spring, from summer to fall,
she uses her five senses

to see, hear, smell,
touch and taste
the things that happen
in the year's turning.

Sally sees spring with the
first flowers, the new leaves.
The fields and woods
turn soft and green.

She hears spring
as the robins sing,
the brooks run,
the frogs trill in the pond.

She smells spring
in daffodils and warm earth.

She touches spring
holding new kittens.

She tastes spring
in syrup from the maple trees,
and makes "sugar on snow."

Spring turns to summer,
warm, beautiful summer,

and Sally sees the hay cut
in the fields.

She hears the cowbells
in the green pastures.

She smells wild roses.

She touches fat puppies,
and their fur is soft.

She tastes wild strawberries
warm in the sun.

Summer changes to fall.

Sally sees bright leaves
against blue sky.

She hears the call of wild geese.

She smells cornstalks
and pumpkins and frost.

She touches smooth new acorns.

She tastes red apples.

Fall becomes winter.

Sally sees the snow
on field and wood.

She hears sleigh bells.

She smells wood smoke
and cold air.

She touches shining
Christmas balls.

She tastes a candy cane,
and Christmas is here.

This is a year in Sally's life,
filled with the special delights
her five senses bring.
These delights can be yours, too,
when you smell a flower,
or hear a bird's song,
or see the stars on a quiet night.
Then, like Sally, you'll know
that the truly wonderful things
in the world are all around you,
waiting for you to find them.

Born in Boston, Tasha Tudor grew up on a farm in Connecticut, and her impressions of rural New England life are the inspiration for her artwork. She has won many awards and honors since her first book was published in 1938. More than sixty books later, her gift is still unique. She now lives in Vermont where she is surrounded by her corgis, her family, and her friends—and the country pleasures so lovingly depicted in her books.